Just in Passing

Just in Passing

BY SUSAN BONNERS

LOTHROP, LEE & SHEPARD BOOKS

NEW YORK

Printed in Hong Kong.

First Edition 1 2 3 4 5 6 7 8 9 10

Library of Congress Cataloging in Publication Data
Bonners, Susan. Just In Passing / Susan Bonners   p.   cm.   Summary: A yawn is
passed from a baby to an enormous number of people, one by one, until it comes back to the
baby. ISBN 0-688-07711-0. ISBN 0-688-07712-9 (lib. bdg.)   [1. Yawning —
Fiction.   2. Stories without words.]   I. Title.   PZ7.B64253Ju   1989   [E] —dc19
88-22021 CIP AC

*To the baby I once saw in passing,
whose magnificent yawn opened up
so many possibilities*

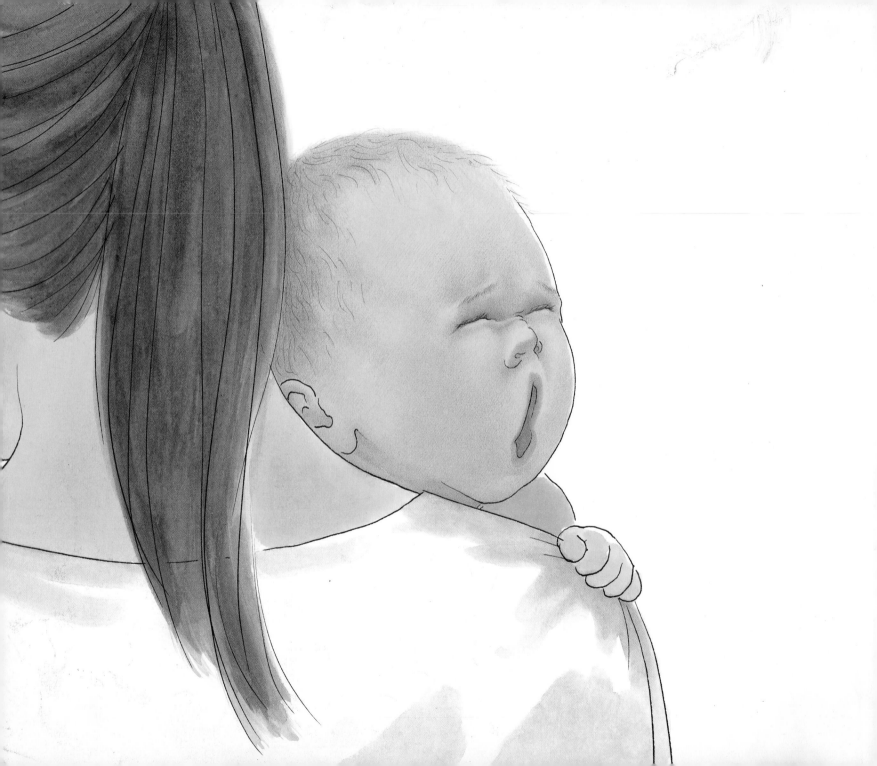

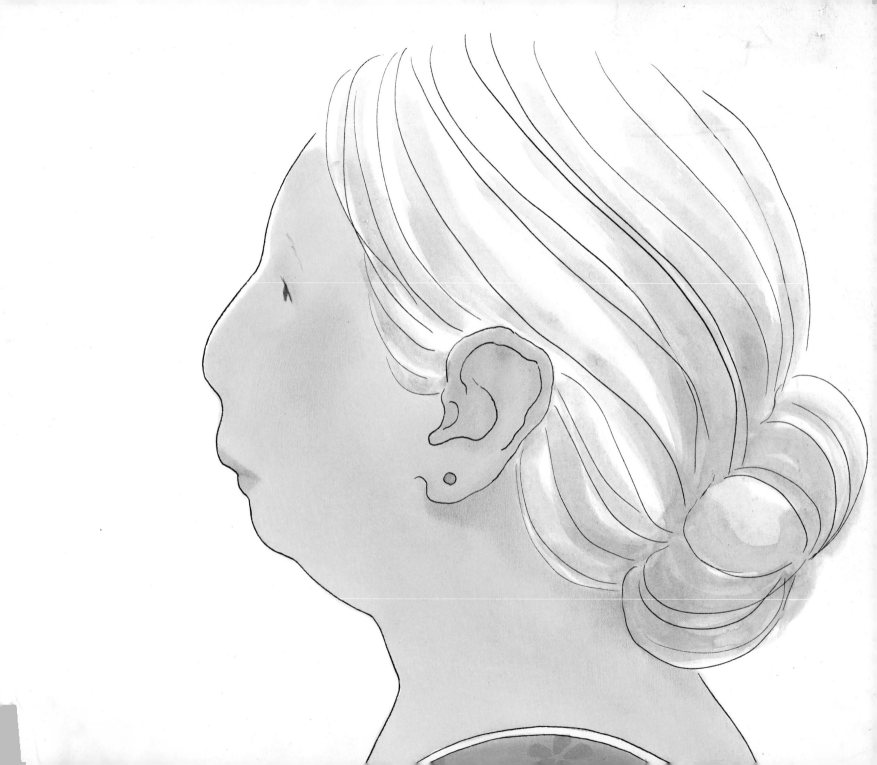